BEYOND
THUNDERING
WATERS

Beyond Thundering Waters

DARK FOLKLORE

Georgina Jeffery

Coblyn Press

I was ten years old when I met the troll.

The peaks of the Utladalen valley were in the grip of winter, and snow lay thick on the mountains and their slopes of open forest. I was walking the road along the river, the one that would eventually lead to the mighty Vettisfossen waterfall a further three miles away.

The bare birch trees lining the path shone bright in the afternoon light; I'd always thought they looked as if someone had painted snow on them. When I was much younger, and first saw them rising out of the deep, icy drifts, I thought perhaps the snow itself had grown into a tree.

I knew the trail very well. Mamma had shown me all the waterfalls along it, and we'd once gotten so close to the foot of Vettisfossen that we were soaked through for the walk home. Now, the smaller falls lay still, entombed in ice.

I was not supposed to be out there alone.

I'd been walking for a long time. My legs ached,

fatigued from pushing through deep snow in my heavy reindeer wellies. Mamma had bought them for me for my last birthday.

I sat down on a bank where green bilberry shoots poked out of the snow and buried my face in my knees. Immediately, I regretted it. Bitter cold seeped in through my waterproof trousers, despite the blinding sun overhead. The sky was blue and empty – a perfect day. It only amplified my loneliness.

'I should just stay here and die of cold,' I told the snow. 'No one would notice.'

'Why is that, poor child?'

I squealed, startled into panic by the voice. 'Who's there?'

Soft titters floated on the air. 'Come into the trees.'

I jumped up and spun in a circle, flinging snow from my coat. 'You better not have spied on me! I wasn't crying, you know!' I glared into the woods with puffy red eyes. The scene was a blur of white and grey.

I thought I saw movement – an indistinct shape that drifted from behind one tree to another.

'Come out!' I said brazenly. 'I can *see* you.'

More quiet laughter. I bristled. 'Did Pappa send you after me? Tell him I don't want to go back! I don't want to live in our house anymore!'

'Why is that, little one?'

'I'm not little!'

'Why is that, loud one?'

'Are you making fun of me?' My voice cracked. I felt the blubbers welling in my throat again. 'That's not fair . . . It's not fair . . .'

The voice drew closer. 'What is not fair, tearful one?'

'*Nothing!*' I screamed. The echo should have bounced off all the mountains, but instead it was absorbed by the cushion of snow. I felt betrayed by my valley. 'Nothing's fair,' I muttered to my feet. 'Mamma's gone . . .'

Something velvety touched my cheek. I looked up, bewildered. Shining golden eyes met mine.

I backed away from the outstretched hand. 'You snuck up on me!'

'You were not paying attention.' There was amusement in the voice. Its owner smiled: a sweet, splendid smile. She was probably the most beautiful woman I had ever seen.

'Aren't you cold?' I said warily. She wore only a

veil-like dress which was wrapped from her shoulders down to her hips, and draped loosely about her pale legs.

'Where has your Mamma gone?' she asked.

'She died.' I stared blankly at her bare feet, which were curiously standing on top of the snow. I glanced down at my own, where my wellies were sunk halfway up to the knees.

'How did she die?'

'She was sick.' The words caught in my throat. 'She died in our– in our house . . .'

Her fingers brushed my cheek again. They looked as white as bone, but her skin was silky soft like the velour of Mamma's winter dresses. 'You miss your Mamma?'

I nodded, and it tipped the weight of tears forward in my head. The stranger held out her arms and I collapsed into them, like it was exactly what I'd been waiting for. Her fingers stroked my hair as my shoulders heaved in ugly sobs. I babbled to her about summers walking the valley with Mamma, about collecting leaves in the autumn and pretending to catch fish in the sparkling river waters in the spring. I told her about long winters curled up in Mamma's lap listening to fairy tales, and days spent baking gingerbread houses followed by evenings drinking hot chocolate by the fire. And I told her about the day she died, when all the family had come from far away to squeeze into our house and sit in silence, while Mamma choked on her own breath in the next room.

'Poor girl,' she said. 'Poor child.'

Eventually I stopped quaking. 'Did Pappa send you?' I asked feebly.

'No.' Her fingers stilled in my hair. 'Your Pappa is alone now?'

'Mm.'

'And you need a Mamma.' Her fingers resumed stroking. 'Poor child. Poor child. So alone. So sad. Home you go now.'

She pushed me gently away and pointed back down the path. 'Home you go,' she repeated, still smiling. 'Pappa is waiting.'

I looked forlornly back the way I had come. Another two hours of trudging awaited me just to reach the edge of town. But I knew there was nowhere else to go.

'Okay,' I said heavily. 'Will you walk with me? What's your name?'

'No. I must go home, too. I am Maja. Goodbye, mournful one.'

As she turned around, the thin material of her dress fluttered open at the back. It revealed an inhuman secret beneath. A sunken cavity in her back, surrounded by bark-like skin, and a tufted tail that flicked up from the base of her spine.

I gasped. She looked coyly over her shoulder and placed a finger to her lips, then continued walking deep into the silver woods.

I don't know if I was shivering from cold or shaking from shock, but I stood rooted for more than ten minutes before my senses returned, along with a burst of adrenaline. I hurled myself down the path, a slow crunching run through snow, in the direction of home. I was blurry-eyed and panting, so I didn't see the figure blocking the road ahead.

I ran into it, shrieked, and started beating my fists against its padded raincoat.

'Ida! Ida, calm down, love. Calm down.' Pappa's voice. 'You worried me, Ida. I was lucky to guess you'd come this way. You shouldn't be out here all alone.'

I didn't even look up, just buried my head in

his chest and whimpered. 'I don't like the house,' I mumbled into his coat.

Pappa sighed deeply and wrapped his arms around me. 'I know, love. It's hard. But it won't always be this way.'

The light was already fading. Pappa carried me most of the way home on his back. By the time we reached our house the sun had disappeared behind the mountains, leaving us in the fuzzy blue-grey of dusk.

We brought wood in from the store, and Pappa made lighting the woodstove his first task. I curled up on the rug in front of it, dripping water from my trousers and sniffling pathetically.

'Here, Ida. Drink up.' Pappa handed me a cup of hot chocolate, sprinkled with cinnamon.

He let me be by the fire. I waited for some retribution for my actions, but it never came. I stared into my drink.

I hated the way I was excused even more than I hated the way people always spoke quietly around us now. Ever since that day, when family I barely knew brought silence into our house ... the silence stayed behind even when they left with their hushed goodbyes trailing after them.

Dinner was Pappa's fish stew, and we ate that in silence too.

I couldn't bear it anymore. I pushed my bowl away.

'Pappa. What kind of things live in the trees on the way to Vettisfossen?'

He looked at me with surprise. 'Lots of animals. Did you see a deer?'

'No. What about people? People with . . . tails? Like a cow's.'

Pappa smiled faintly. 'Oh? One of Mamma's stories? Let me think now . . . that might be a troll you're thinking of.'

'She was too pretty to be a troll.'

'Met one, did you?'

'Yes. She had long golden hair.'

'I bet she did.'

'And golden eyes.'

'Wonderful.'

'And her back had a hole in it.'

Pappa's brow creased. 'A hole?'

'She looked like a tree!' I burst out, flinging my spoon down on the table. 'As if her back was made of bark, but it was hollow like the inside of a tree!'

The light of recognition dawned on his face.

'Aha, I know that one. It sounds like a huldra. She *is* a type of troll. Or at least, I think that was how your Mamma told it.' He trailed off, staring blankly at the wall for a moment. His face looked more worn than it used to. Sadness always hung about his pinched lips and drawn features now.

His eyes swung back to me and a smile was forced for my benefit. 'Well now, what were you doing with a huldra in the woods? I hope you didn't leave the path – you know it can be danger-ous, especially at this time of year.'

I leaned forward over the table and whispered. 'She came out of the trees. We just talked.'

'About what?'

I hesitated. 'About Mamma. About the house.'

Part of me expected him to flinch or to sigh, but he gave no reaction at all. Perhaps he'd antici-pated it.

'Do you think it really was a troll, Pappa?' I pressed. 'What if she was a spirit? Do you think Mamma's a spirit? What if Mamma is still here?'

Now he was rattled. 'Then she'll keep us safe. That's enough talk of trolls and ghosts for tonight. Finish your dinner, then off to bed with you.'

* * *

I thought little of the huldra for the rest of winter. There was the question of school to be addressed, and the nagging urgency of my return. It all had to go back to normal I was told, now that the funeral was dealt with and I'd had my 'little time away'. But my classmates were quiet and my friends quieter around me. The house was quiet. Pappa was quiet.

I was also quiet. I spent most of the term staring bleakly out of classroom windows. This was our new normal.

Winter rolled into spring. The valley became less white, the woods less silver. Green took hold and the sun started to feel warm again. Summer began to feel less like a misremembered dream and more like a truth on the horizon as the tourists trickled in to our small town of Øvre Årdal.

The people came for the scenery, and to conquer the valley: its mountains, the river, and its waterfalls. Being nestled in such a tree-ridden landscape, you wouldn't think that our town was also home to the aluminium smelting plant where

Pappa worked. When the wind blew in the right direction it carried chemical odours through the leaves, and sometimes you'd see hikers wrinkling their noses as they set off in the dull morning light.

Pappa came home from work tired every day. He used to always have a smile for Mamma and me, but these days it was as if he didn't have the energy to smile at all.

That is, until one hot day in April, when he greeted me home from school.

'Why are you home early, Pappa?' I asked him with puzzlement.

He gave me a wide, enthusiastic smile. It should have made me feel warm, but it didn't. Something about it told me that he was nervous. 'I have something to tell you, Ida.'

I dropped my school bags sullenly. 'What is it?'

'Now, I don't want you to get angry.'

'Why would I get angry?'

'And I don't want you to be upset.'

'Why would I–?'

'I've met someone, Ida,' he said firmly. 'You're going to have a new mother.'

'What?' The word clawed inside my throat and forced its way out again as a shriek. '*What?*'

'Don't be upset, Ida.'

I wanted to scream. I wanted to smash my fists on the floor. I wanted to howl the whole house down with *no, never, you can't! I won't!*

'That's *wrong*,' I choked.

His eyes crinkled with sympathy. But there was also a deep furrow in his brow, like he was struggling to process my reaction. What had he been expecting?

'I know this is hard,' he said. 'No one will ever replace your Mamma in my heart. But I need you to understand. I can't go on alone, Ida.'

'*She only just died!*' I pushed him away as he tried to reach out.

Now he crumpled, falling into a chair and expelling a long breath. The gauntness of his cheeks reminded me horribly of Mamma for a second. He rubbed his temples while avoiding my furious gaze. 'Surely you understand a little, Ida. Mamma was barely with us towards the end. She'd already disappeared so long before then . . .'

I refused to acknowledge the truth of this. 'Not even a year!' I yelled through tears. 'She's not even been gone a year!'

'We need to move on . . .' Pappa's voice faltered, as though even he wasn't convinced by his own words. He opened his arms again, like he thought I would allow him to hug me. 'Ida, please calm down–'

'*No!*'

I shoved past him, wrenched open the front door and flew out of it. I sprinted down calm streets all the way to the tree line on the edge of town, and didn't stop until I was completely hidden from view. Hot rage simmered in my chest.

My lungs hitched in frantic gasps as I stumbled unsteadily through the woods, in any direction. Leaves and branches whipped my face. Every slap and pinch of foliage fanned my anger.

I didn't hear the rushing water until I was on top of it.

I stopped short of slipping down the bank. The river gushed below, tumbling thick and fast with the weight of a winter's worth of melted snow. It would eventually feed the colossal lake that butted against the edge of Øvre Årdal and sealed us into the valley. We were surrounded on all sides by mountains and water, walls and moats. Utladalen was a trap. We would never leave.

I sank to my knees in the dirt, too angry to cry anymore. I slumped sideways against a tree. 'I hate him,' I muttered.

'Hate who, vexed one?'

I looked up, briefly dazzled by sunlight until a shadow blocked it. In its wake stood the huldra, smiling faintly as her thin dress fluttered in the spring breeze.

'I knew you were real,' I breathed. In the back of my mind I wondered if she was standing where a tree had been just moments before.

She spread her hands. 'Who upsets you, troubled child?'

'Pappa,' I said instantly. I rose, fists-clenched and trembling. 'He's done something evil. He wants to replace Mamma! He's seeing some other . . . some other *woman*. I won't let him!'

The huldra tilted her head quizzically. 'But the sad child wanted a new Mamma?'

'No, I didn't!' I screamed. Then caught myself, ashamed for shouting at her. 'Sorry. Pappa is doing a horrid thing.'

She nodded slowly. 'You do not like your Pappa.'

'I don't,' I said vehemently. 'In fact, I don't want to see him ever again. I hate him. *I hate him!*'

'Poor child,' crooned the huldra. She came towards me with her arms outstretched. 'You don't need a Pappa. You're with Maja, now.'

She pulled me into a hug. Her skin was very cold.

'Maybe I could come live with you.' I sniffled into her neck. 'That would really teach him.'

I felt her smile against my head.

'No, child. You cannot come with Maja.'

'Where do you live?'

She pointed down the length of the valley. 'Behind the thundering waters.'

'You mean the Vettisfossen?'

She didn't answer, instead brushing the hair out of my face. 'Humans cannot go there.'

'What happens if they do?'

'They drown.'

'. . . Oh.'

She turned me round, facing away from the surging river. 'Home now, child. Maja will fix everything.'

'You will?' My feet obeyed, despite my confusion. 'What will you do?' I called over my shoulder.

The huldra smiled, and within a blink I'd lost sight of her among the trees.

I shuddered away the goosebumps and made my way home.

My deep wells of fury dissipated over the walk, and by the time the village came back into sight I'd sunk into a much shallower pool of depression.

The front door banged opened to announce my return. The house was dark and cold. I shuffled awkwardly on the threshold, thrown off by unexpected shadows warping the shape of the room.

'Well, I'm home,' I muttered. I fumbled for the light switch and moved on tiptoe through the house as though Pappa was waiting to pounce on me from around the next corner. He did not.

I shivered in the empty kitchen. The sky was dark outside. I hated the way the night pressed up against the windows.

Probably Pappa was in bed, even though it was early. Or maybe he'd gone for a walk. Maybe he'd gone to see his – I conjured up the worst swear word I knew – his *bitch.*

My cheeks went red. Mamma would have frowned if she heard me say that aloud. I thought

of her spirit in the house and made a silent apology
to the walls.

After staring blankly into the fridge for a while,
I fixed myself a plate of cold food while inwardly
sulking that Pappa hadn't left anything out for me.
I ate on the sofa while curled up in a blanket – a
luxury usually reserved for Sundays – while watch-
ing my favourite cartoon, Ivan the Reindeer, until
long past my bedtime. As the time ticked closer to
10 PM, I felt a tightening in my stomach. It was
a horrible gnawing feeling, like if worry was an
animal. Or, possibly, just the cold ham I'd eaten.

I left all the lights on downstairs when I finally
tramped up to bed. I'd never been left on my own
for a night before. I thought I'd gotten used to
silence, but now it scared me.

Pappa's bedroom was opposite mine. Chewing
my lip, I nudged open the door.

The bed was tidy, the room spartan, as it had
been since Mamma went. Pappa had boxed up
most of her things, like he was trying to erase her
from the house. I wondered if he still felt her next
to him when he went to sleep. Then I wondered
if the horrible Other Woman would sleep in this
bed. It made me feel sick.

I slammed the door harder than I intended and the sound made me jump.

'Sorry Mamma,' I whispered to the house.

I snuck guiltily into bed. Pappa would usually have me asleep an hour ago. Why wasn't he back yet?

The Other Woman loomed large in my imagination, an ugly apparition with hooked nose and hairy warts, sneering at me with a broken-toothed grin. Instantly she was the Evil Stepmother and I the abused servant-child forced to obey her every whim. She was a witch, maybe, from one of Mamma's stories, and had put Pappa under a nasty spell. We were both slaves to her evil power, and that's why Pappa wasn't home.

I cried into my pillow.

I'd never had to eat dinner alone before. Sometimes in the past, Pappa would have to work very late. But it had never mattered because Mamma would always be at home instead. Except, now she wasn't.

BOOM.

I jerked upright. The sound rattled the windows – and my teeth. It was like a peel of thunder, but at ground level. My body juddered with it for three seconds, four, five . . . and by then it had faded into echoes bouncing off the mountains.

I sat extremely still in this new, terrifying silence. My heart thudded so hard it was painful. It sounded like a drum in my ears. I could barely catch my breath.

Later, there were sirens. Blue lights flashed past my window.

I lay with the covers pulled up over my face and trembled alone in the dark.

* * *

The space between falling asleep and waking up felt invisible.

Pale grey light filtered through my curtains. 6:00 AM blinked from my Ivan the Reindeer alarm clock. I squinted at the ceiling as my brain took in the sounds from outside. There was the rumble of large vehicles and the distant shouts of many voices. It had a matter-of-fact quality to it, the sombre tones of people getting a job done. I blearily wondered if it was builders, and why they had to start work so early.

I padded out of my bedroom in pyjamas. Pappa's room was still empty, untouched. I hugged myself tightly. He was probably just downstairs making breakfast. Probably he'd come in late and not wanted to disturb me. He would have slept on the sofa.

I started cautiously downstairs, scared of finding it still empty. But halfway down I was relieved to hear humming coming from the kitchen. I ran the rest of the way and stopped dead at the bottom. It was a woman's voice.

Ice gripped my throat. I couldn't believe Pappa would have brought her here. I didn't want to meet her.

I entered the kitchen slowly. A woman stared out of the window, humming a gentle tune I'd never heard before. She appeared to notice my presence and turned around.

The world stood still.

I knew that face. That curly dark hair. That slightly lopsided smile. The ice in my blood splintered; a million shards exploded in my chest. My entire soul ached to see her again.

'Mamma?' I keened.

She nodded and held her arms open.

I ran into them, already sobbing. I clutched at her soft velvety dress and buried my nose in it, desperate for her faintly flowery perfume and smell of the apple soap she used.

I knew it must be a dream, but I wasn't willing to relinquish it easily. She felt so real as she stroked my hair. Her voice was a music I'd been craving with anguish. Everything about her was home, was comfort, was safe.

'Poor child,' she said softly. 'Sad child. No more tears, forlorn one.'

I went stiff. This was not what I wanted in my dream.

'I just want Mamma,' I said quietly.

'I am your Mamma, sorrowful one.'

I pulled away and looked up. Golden eyes filled my vision. 'You're Maja. Get out of my dream, Maja.'

She held a delicate hand to Mamma's mouth. 'Silly child. You are awake. Here.' In a snake-fast strike she caught my cheek between two fingers and pinched hard.

'*Ow!*' I stumbled backwards while she tittered. More tears welled up with the pain. 'That was mean! Why did you do that?'

'Maja teaches the child what is real. The poor child is awake. Mamma teaches.'

'You're not my Mamma!'

She smiled, so kindly. 'Poor child. Confused child. Doesn't know what it wants. Mamma will look after you.'

'*You're not my Mamma.* Stop looking like her! I'll tell Pappa what you are, then you'll be sorry!'

She tilted her head. 'Pappa is gone.'

'He's coming back.'

'No, he is not.'

I stared at her open, honest face. Mamma's face was always honest.

'What have you done with him?' My voice was hoarse. It mounted into a shrill, pleading wail. 'You better not have done anything to him!'

She shrugged. 'Pappa was horrid. Pappa was evil. The child did not want to see Pappa ever again.'

'I didn't mean it!' I rushed to say. 'I take it back! What have you done? *What have you done?*'

'Hush, child.'

'No! *No! N–!*'

My screech of pain was muffled between pinched lips. The huldra's nails dug into my skin.

'Hush,' she said sweetly. She towered over me in Mamma's form, no longer the diminutive creature I'd met in the woods. 'Poor child. Ungrateful child. Maja gives you everything you ask. The child wants a new Mamma for her Pappa . . . Maja provides. But the child does not want this new Mamma. The child does not want a Pappa. Maja provides. The child is still ungrateful. What *does* the child want?'

I couldn't speak, held hostage by her vice-grip on my lips. The huldra smiled down at me, but it lacked any of the warmth in Mamma's face.

'Maja will give what the child *needs*. Poor child. Lost child. Sad child. I will make you happy. I will be your Mamma, child.'

Tears dripped from my chin. I was scared her nails might pierce right through my mouth. But then she withdrew her fingers and opened her arms again.

'Come to Mamma, child.'

I nearly froze. But I remembered that the path to the door was right behind me. I bolted.

A faint sigh trailed after me. 'Foolish child . . .'

I wrenched open the front door and sprung out of it, still dressed in only slippers and pyjamas. I ran halfway down the street before I had to stop, choking on the dusty air.

A grey pall hung over the village. It came with a cloying metallic smell. I looked up and saw columns of smoke in the distance, rising and spreading across the sky like a dirty stain. It looked as though it could latch onto the mountains and roll a black ceiling over our heads.

I remembered the sound of thunder last night. I started to shake. The smoke was coming from the aluminium plant. Was Pappa . . . ?

Trucks passed me, heading in the same direction. Some carried diggers or had small cranes attached.

For lifting rubble, I thought dizzily.

I started to run.

I waved madly at the trucks as they passed me, shouting as loud as I could. One slowed and a frowning man stuck his head out the window.

'What's up, kid? You shouldn't be out here.'

'My Pappa,' I gasped. 'He works at the factory!

What happened? Was there an explosion? *Is Pappa okay?'*

The man's expression changed. He pulled his truck over beside me. 'You got other family here, kid? Where do you live?'

I shook my head frantically. 'Can you take me to–'

A cold hand gripped my shoulder.

'There you are, child,' said the huldra, in a voice as soft and wispy as her dress. Her thumb jabbed cruelly into the back of my neck. 'I will take you home now.'

'No! Mister, please–' A hole formed in my stomach, sucking all my breath inwards as I perceived the way the truck driver looked at the huldra. He was slack-jawed, suddenly vacant behind the eyes. It didn't seem like he could hear me. He was transfixed on the huldra.

She didn't look like Mamma anymore. She was barefoot on the tarmac in a dress as solid as net curtains, with her wild hair glowing in the pale morning sun. I stared numbly at her long tufted tail, which was in plain sight.

The man in the truck, he stared too. He was absorbed in her golden eyes.

The huldra smiled, for once with an open mouth, revealing sharp teeth resting behind her lips. Her tail flicked behind her. 'I will take the child home.'

The man nodded vaguely. 'Right you are. Keep safe, kid.'

The truck drove away and the huldra turned me back towards the house.

I twisted in her grip. It sent shooting pains from my shoulder into my spine.

'Home now,' she said.

'What have you done to Pappa?' I tried pleading. 'Was he in the explosion? Please say you haven't killed him. Please say he isn't dead.'

She stopped, eyebrows raised in what could be genuine surprise. 'No. I would not kill Pappa. I am a good Mamma.'

I gulped with nauseous relief. 'He wasn't in the explosion?'

'No. But everyone else will think otherwise.'

I writhed again. 'Where is he? What have you done with him?'

She seemed to relent and relaxed her hold for a moment. 'I sent him away. Pappa is gone to the land of the huldra.'

My face screwed up as I exclaimed in horror, 'But you said humans can't come back from there! *You said we drown.*' I finally wrenched free. 'Please! Please let me have my Pappa back! Don't let him drown! Please! Please!'

The huldra frowned deeply. It was exactly the sad frown that Mamma would wear when I upset her. 'Hush, despairing one. Pappa is already on his way. Is this not what you asked for?'

I clasped my hands together as if praying – I *was* praying, to her. 'Please! I'll do anything! I won't do or say anything bad ever again. I won't swear. I won't complain about Pappa's fish stew. I'll stop asking to move house. I'll be the best daughter. *Please.*'

She leaned down so that we were nose to nose. 'You will be *my* daughter?'

The question chilled me to the core. 'Yes.'

She bounced lightly on her heels. There was a glint in her eyes. 'It is a long way to the thundering waters. You must get there before sundown, or you will not catch Pappa in time.' She paused and tilted her head – it struck me how animal-like the gesture was. She looked amused. 'You should run, child.'

My stomach dropped into my feet. They were suddenly heavy, but I spurred them into a run towards the Utladalsvegen road and the river path that would take me all the way to Vettisfossen.

Our neighbours were still waking up, and those who were already on the streets were entirely preoccupied with the aluminium plant. I might as well have been invisible as I galloped to the edge of town, running right alongside the fencing to the factory where the coil of black, oily smoke marred the sky. I stopped, partly for the dust that made me gag, and partly for the throbbing stitch in my sides.

My tears pattered onto the road. It sunk in that I was suddenly, entirely, by myself. There would be no smiling stranger in the woods to comfort me this time; there would be no Pappa to come out searching for me with worry painted all over his face; and there would never ever be Mamma, my real Mamma, there to pull me into a tight hug and tell me that everything was going to be okay.

There was just me. Ida. Alone on the road by a smouldering factory.

I rubbed my eyes. They felt red and sore, and barely wet. Probably I'd run out of tears. I was fed up with crying.

I stared at the road ahead. It was familiar, yet hostile. There would be tarmac for several miles, and normally I'd take at least two hours to walk it. After that it was a rough path through trees and over steep, uneven ground – another two hours to get all the way to Vettisfossen.

Mamma and I would make a whole day of it, take a picnic with us, and have many rest stops. We'd leave early in the morning, almost as early as it was now, and then we'd approach home just as the sun was setting, stretching its golden arms over the lake.

I'd never walked all the way to Vettisfossen on my own. I'd never made it past the second waterfall, even.

Pappa was out there, somewhere. Stolen by my valley. Stolen by the huldra. I'd walk all day if I had to. I had to hurry.

My slippers were damp, but they were better than nothing on the hard road. Ivan the Reindeer grinned up at me with every step. I jogged for as long as I could, then walked a while, then jogged again. I counted the steps of each. One hundred. Fifty. Ninety-five. Sixty-two. Eighty-one. Seventy . . . Gradually my jogs shortened, and the walks lengthened. The sun climbed above my head, scaring away the shadows from the trees.

Eventually I came to the foot of Hjellefossen, the first waterfall on the trail, and knew the tar-macked road would be running out soon. I paused on the bridge to catch my breath and turned my face towards the falls, willing some of the spray to rise up and hit my cheeks. The path was really too far away from the water, but the air around it was cool and lifted some of the sweat from my skin.

The lull only brought new pains to my attention. My stomach was achingly empty. It seemed a trifling concern next to my quest to save Pappa from the huldra, but the thought occurred that everything would be a lot easier on a slice of toast.

I staggered over the bridge and caught a glimpse of dark blue spots just off the beaten path ahead. My heart leapt with hope. The season was too early for bilberries – they shouldn't fruit until the very end of summer. But as my feet took me further and further away from the path it was obvious my eyes weren't mistaken. They were definitely bilberries, and it was a whole bush of them, looking full and round and ripe like they'd been put there just for me.

I descended on them in a frenzy. I grabbed handfuls off their stalks and shoved them in my mouth. Purple juice stained my hands and pyjamas. I plucked berry after berry after berry until I'd nearly stripped the whole bush and I felt fuller and more content than I had in months.

I sat down. The sun was warm and pleasant through the dappled shade of the trees. I knew I had to keep walking, but my legs were so heavy. A short rest wouldn't hurt. And I couldn't quite remember what I had been walking for.

From somewhere deeper in the woods, the sound of a woman singing drifted on the air. It was soft and calm like a lullaby and was perfect for such a peaceful moment. My eyelids weighed heavy. The sun was so warm.

I swear I only blinked.

I looked up and the sky was a deep, mean orange. Thoughts of Pappa rushed back into my brain.

'No!' I leapt to my feet and shouted at the mountains. 'That's not fair! *That's not fair!*'

There was no bilberry bush where I'd been sat. I rubbed my eyes but it didn't reappear. And I was *starving*.

'That was a dirty trick,' I snarled.

The initial urge to cry was overwhelmed by indignation. I seethed. I wouldn't let the huldra beat me. I *would* reach Pappa in time.

I found a long birch stick in the undergrowth and gripped it purposefully. It was no sword, but it was the best I had.

'Got to run,' I whispered.

I braced. Then sprang.

I'd never been a fast runner. I came last in nearly every race at school. But I always walked lots with Mamma. We hiked through our valley in every weather. And Mamma said endurance was better than speed. She said I had good stamina. Strong legs and good stamina.

I repeated it to myself as I ran. Strong legs and good stamina. I needed to reach Vettisfossen before the sun set fully, but it would be no good if I collapsed halfway there. I had to keep going.

The road merged into a gravel track following the River Utla, curving North-East. Mud caked my blackened slippers as I hurried on to the roaring Avdalfossen. It crossed my mind that the water-falls seemed like tremendous gates I had to pass through to reach my goal. And as I approached this one, it scared me.

The sound of it crashed in my ears. It fell in foaming white rivulets that tumbled down the mountainside. It was just water. But it could cut great rifts in a mountain. *It could wash me away,* I thought.

As though it had heard me, the waterfall swelled. It flooded down the mountain in a sudden torrent; it burst the banks of the river and washed over the trail ahead of me. I stumbled back. My path was shrouded in a cloud of churning water. It frothed like the mouth of a mad thing.

I turned to shout at the Avdalfossen. 'Traitor!' I screamed. 'What would Mamma think of you?'

I didn't care to see if it had heard me. I closed my eyes and marched into the foam, holding my hands up against the spray that gushed like torren-tial rain in my face. I gripped my birch stick tight, and speared it into the ground as an anchor when I was nearly pushed over. The water pelted me like little bullets, bruising with the force of hailstones. Slowly, painfully slowly, I put one foot in front of the other. *I can endure this,* I promised.

The water fell away as I emerged beyond its reach. It drained away into the dirt, retreating to its original course.

Now shivering, I struggled onward and lost a slipper to the mud. I tossed the other sodden slipper away as well. Barefoot would be easier, anyway. The huldra wouldn't beat me in my own valley.

My toes dug into the soil. I felt like a wild thing. Fiercely connected to the trees and waters that made up my home. I could feel every lump and crevice under my feet, every root that snaked across the path as I advanced grimly on while the sky turned red. These roots were my roots. The huldra wouldn't lay claim to any of it, least of all my Pappa.

Soon I saw Holjafossen, the third thundering gate. It was low and squat compared to its sister falls. Not nearly as powerful as the others. But I wouldn't be fooled this time.

I slunk forward cautiously. My footsteps were soft as silk; toes curled like claws around stones buried in the mud to keep my footing. I prodded the next patch of ground with my swordstick. It sunk by more than a foot into the mire.

It was then that I realised the Holjafossen's trick. Mud squelched over my ankles as I began to sink. I wriggled and squirmed to drag one foot up – but with a sucking *plop* it was forced back into the muck.

The rage in my chest burned like a furnace. It fired strength into my muscles, pouring molten steel into my arms and my hands where I gripped the swordstick. I wrenched it free with a howl of exertion. Reams of sweat cascaded down my back, meeting the mud that encroached up my legs. I was knee-deep and panting like an animal.

There were large rocks nearby. If I could reach them . . .

First I threw the stick. It landed safely on the stones. Then I threw myself bodily, using the whole length of my torso to close the distance. My fingertips worked into jagged edges. My nails, normally bitten raw, seemed to hook into cracks like talons until I was secure in my hold.

Again I willed my fury into steel. The muscles in my arms burned with the strain until I thought they might snap. But, inch my inch, I dragged myself out of the Holjafossen's bog-trap.

I sprawled over the rocks, wheezing for air. Behind me, Holjafossen's gentle bubbling was jarringly peaceful.

'Three down,' I said, and it came out as more of a hiss than I'd intended.

I picked up my swordstick and found my footing on the rocks. I could avoid the mud if I went from stone to stone.

I crawled on all fours, stretching limbs between landing places. The path turned to dirt track through the trees. When Holjafossen was out of sight I felt safer in my footing, and began galloping up the steep and rocky path.

The sun was already well behind the mountains, robbing the valley of its vibrant colours. I ran through a drained world, leaping over faded tree roots and navigating more by the sound of the river than the hazy sight of it.

The roar of tons of crashing water reached my ears. Vettisfossen couldn't be much further. My thigh muscles burned. My swordstick found more use as a walking stick – I was struggling to lift my legs over the rocks. There were barely any trees now on the steep slopes, but I could hear the huldra's light laughter floating down the valley.

I picked myself up again. It had been hard when Mamma and I walked this trail. But we'd laughed and joked and thrown stones in the river and stopped for cheese sandwiches by the friendly Holjafossen. I remembered the first time we got this far, I threw a tantrum because the path was too steep and my feet hurt.

Mamma waited for me to calm down, then she asked me, 'Do you want to go home? Or do you want to finish what we started?'

We finished the trail. Seeing the Vettisfossen for the first time was the most magical moment I could remember. It was like meeting a character out of her stories. Mamma told me that 'Vetti' meant fairy tale meadow. She always talked about it.

The waterfall came into view.

It was a single torrent of foaming white water, pouring over the edge of a cliff like it was coming out of a tap. Its thunder was near deafening as I picked my way closer along the bank. There was only the barest trace of pink left in the sky.

'Pappa!' I shouted into the spray. *'Pappa!'*

There was no sign of him.

I filled my lungs and bellowed into the sky. *'I'm here! I made it on time! Let me have my Pappa!'*

The sound of Vettisfossen died away. It was still there, but as though someone had turned the volume down. A new rushing noise caught my attention from the middle of the frothing basin that the waterfall emptied into.

The churning water suddenly churned *upwards*, like a slowly erupting geyser. The column of water tumbled away to reveal Pappa, soaking and unconscious, laid out on a bed of floating pebbles.

'Give him back,' I told the water.

'Kiss your Mamma first, child.'

The huldra appeared like a ghost, glowing almost white in the grey dusk-light. But my eyes adjusted, and she became just a pale woman in a pale dress.

'I want my Pappa first,' I snarled, and it was a real, feral snarl from my throat that shocked me into silence.

'Mamma is proud,' said the huldra. 'So strong, is her daughter.'

'I am not your daughter!' I roared. As I did,

I clenched my fists and felt the bite of nails into my skin. I opened my hands and stared at them in numb disbelief. Sharp claws extended from my fingertips.

My toes curled involuntarily into the dirt, and there too I could feel some new part of me that was not mine. Glancing down, where mud caked my shins, I saw not mud but brown velvet fur covering my legs. With a horrified squeak, I registered the swish of a tail at my back.

The huldra sauntered closer, arms wide open. 'Child. So much I've had to do to bring you here. Don't you miss me? Won't you come home with me?'

There. She was my mother again, right in front of me. Curly hair, lopsided smile. She'd told me so many stories about the falls. About the huldra. About the hidden creatures of our valley. Would it be so silly to think . . . ?

Her name escaped my lips. 'Mamma . . . ?'

The huldra's mouth twisted. Proud joy or cruel triumph? I couldn't tell. Flecks of gold flashed in her eyes.

My gaze swung from her to Pappa, and back again.

Do you want to go home?

Her arms reached for me.

Or do you want to finish what you started?

'I came here for my Pappa,' I said defiantly, 'and I'm taking him home.'

'We shall go home together.'

'No,' I hissed through pointed teeth. 'You're not my Mamma. Mamma was never cruel. She wouldn't allow you to do this.'

Her face contorted. 'Child–'

'I know you aren't my Mamma, because she isn't gone. You can't replace her because she's still here! She's still *right here!*'

The river began to froth again.

'Silly stories,' the huldra hissed back. 'Poor child. So confused. That Mamma is gone forever.'

'No,' I shouted. 'She's all of this. She's the mountains and the sky and the trees! She's Vettis-fossen and the water itself! You can't take her out of here.' I looked over at Pappa's body in the river. 'And I know she won't let you take Pappa away. I won't let you.'

'Nasty child. It will be punished for telling lies.'

She swooped toward me, sharp nails and

sharper teeth revealed. I thrust out my swordstick like a weapon. I felt it make contact, but not like it had gone through a solid thing.

I let go and stepped back, staring in horror at where the stick pierced the huldra's stomach. Her face transformed with pain and astonishment.

Slowly, she pulled the stick out. Leafmould and insects poured from her middle, accompanied by the smell of decay. Her pale skin cracked, turning white and silvery like the bark of a birch tree. Green leaves sprouted in her hair then withered in the space of a second. She opened her mouth to scream, but by then it was already being swallowed by bark; her whole body consumed by the growth of a thick, woody skin. Her wide eyes fixed on me in the last moments. Glaring. Or pleading?

They blazed golden one last time before falling closed, sealed shut.

And then suddenly it was just another birch tree at the foot of Vettisfossen, with a hole in its trunk at about the height where a mouth might be, caught in an endless scream.

The velvety hairs on my skin bristled all over. My tail quivered as I stared at the tree. What if she had been . . . ?

The fine spray of water on my face brought me back into focus. There was no time to waste in being afraid anymore.

'Let me have my Pappa!' I shouted to the roiling Vettisfossen. I couldn't see Pappa's body in the water any more. 'It's my fault he's here, so I've come to bring him home! I won't leave without him!'

'Who are you talking to, Ida?'

I swivelled, and there was Pappa on the path behind me. I craned up to see his eyes. Not golden. He just looked damp, and a bit confused. I ran up and hugged him ferociously.

'I love you, Pappa.'

He opened and closed his mouth a bit, then said, 'I love you too, Ida. Why are you all the way out here?'

I looked up at him and now, finally, the tears came. 'There was an explosion at the factory. I can't lose you, too. Please, Pappa. Please.'

'Oh, Ida.' He lifted me up, and I could smell dust and smoke and sweat on him, like he'd just come straight from work, and not been lying in the middle of a river for hours at all. 'Ida, I'm so sorry you were scared. I'm here, though. I'm fine. You had me so worried when I couldn't find you.'

'I'm sorry,' I said, and meant it. Then I pulled back, frantically grabbing at the air behind me.

Pappa caught my wrists and bent to my level. 'What's wrong? Are you hurt?'

'No . . .' I couldn't find the tail, and my fingernails were stubby once more. I looked down and saw dried mud on my legs.

Pappa rubbed my shoulders. 'Come home, love. It's a long way to walk.'

I held Pappa's hand the whole way. It got dark fast. We picked our way carefully by the bright light on Pappa's phone, and by the full moon that hung over the valley. We met more people on the way – men and women from town. They'd been out searching for me all day, they said.

A car was waiting at Hjellefossen. *We've passed back through all the gates,* I thought to myself.

One of Pappa's friends came to drive us home. Pappa squeezed my hand as we drove past the still-smouldering aluminium plant. A metallic tang still hung on the breeze.

'Are you hungry?' was the first thing he said to me when we stepped into our home.

'Starving,' I admitted.

'Shower first,' he suggested. 'Get warm, and into some clean clothes.'

I was still in my pyjamas, now muddy and torn up to my knees. It was a relief to get out of them, and to soak away my memories of the day in hot water.

I came down in a fluffy dressing gown, wearing a pair of Mamma's old pink slippers that were too big for my feet, but which gave the delightful feeling that I was walking on pillows. I stopped at the bottom of the stairs, hearing voices at the front door. Pappa was talking to a woman.

My blood froze.

I sidled closer, until I could see the outline of her head beyond his.

'Are you sure you don't want me to stay?' she was saying.

'It's been a hard day,' Pappa replied in a weary voice. With a pang, I knew it was weariness I had caused. 'Ida needs some time to process everything. She just needs time.'

'So long as you're okay, too. If you need anything– Oh.'

Both heads turned as they caught sight of me.

'Oh, Ida,' said Pappa. His expression became anxious as he gestured towards the woman at the door. 'This is . . . this is . . .'

Golden eyes! I thought, panicked.

But no, it was just the way the light had reflected off them for a split-second. As she tilted her head, they became a pleasant hazel colour instead. Her hair was brown. Her face was freckled.

'. . . this is Maria,' Pappa finally got out. 'I didn't mean to introduce you this way. Don't be upset.'

The ice reached my heart, but I knew now that it was just fear. Fear of forgetting Mamma. Fear of losing Pappa to someone else.

'I'm not,' I said quietly.

'Hello,' said Maria. She smiled awkwardly. 'Your Pappa tells me lots of good things about you.'

'Mmhmm.' I leaned sideways, trying to get a better view.

The woman glanced over her shoulder. 'What are you looking for?'

'A tail,' I said, satisfied there wasn't one. 'You can come in if you want. But I won't call you Mamma, and you mustn't *ever* hurt Pappa. Understand?'

They exchanged glances, using the kind of

raised eyebrows that adults like to convey all sorts of secret messages, but which also made them look surprised in a really silly way.

Maria smiled at me, and it seemed like an honest smile, if a bit lopsided. 'Your Pappa's lucky he's got you looking out for him.'

'Yes,' I said simply. I shrugged and turned around. 'I'm making hot chocolate. I'll get three mugs if you're coming in.'

Behind me I heard them continue murmuring.

'I think she might come round to you,' said Pappa.

'What was all that about a tail?'

'She's . . . just working through things in her own way. She has a very active imagination. Takes after her mother.'

'She must miss her terribly.'

'Yes. We just need to give her some time.'

I felt I could hear her smile. Then when she answered, there was an odd inflection in her voice which made me drop the mugs; they shattered on the floor. With a hint of teeth and snow in her voice, she said:

'Poor child.'

About the Author

Georgina Jeffery is a British author of speculative fiction. Her stories often blend elements of fantasy, humour, and horror, and tend to reflect her fascination with folklore from around the world. You'll find mythical beasties, malevolent spirits, and eldritch magic in a lot of her writing.

Georgina's work can be found in a variety of anthologies and journals, including *The NoSleep Podcast*, *Unbreakable Ink*, *The San Cicaro Experience*, and *Copperfield Review Quarterly*.

ALSO BY GEORGINA JEFFERY

The Jack Hansard Series: Season One

Funny urban fantasy with a lot of British folklore. Jack Hansard, occult salesman, turns reluctant detective when his merchandise is stolen and becomes embroiled in a supernatural kidnapping case.

The Jack Hansard Series: Season Two

Jack Hansard and his coblyn friend Ang are back in business. Together they face shapeshifters, piskies, and ancient magics in their quest to track down Ang's missing kin and uncover the secrets of Baines & Grayle.

Within Trembling Caverns (Dark Folklore)

A dark fairy tale in a modern Polish setting. A grandmother cares for an ailing dragon . . . but her compassion places her own family in the jaws of danger.

Across Screaming Seas (Dark Folklore)

A dark fairy tale in a modern Welsh setting. A diver finds herself trapped in a mermaid's lair, wrestling against her own conscience and the need to survive.

The Hub

A supernatural short story with a sci-fi edge. When an app developer accidentally creates a maliciously benevolent social media network, only her girlfriend can save her from what she's brought to life

Lightning Source UK Ltd.
Milton Keynes UK
UKHW010453090223
416681UK00008B/2423